The Glow

Story and illustrations
Copyright Cannon Law
Group,PLLC2020
All rights reserved.

For information and
resources please visit
www.happyworldbooks.net

Special thanks to
Cole Cannon
and
Merrianne Monson

For Sapphire

the
Glow
By Shannon Cannon

God held the glow
from which all life
was made

and They started
by splitting
the night
from the day.

They split the glow more
making land,
making sea

and continued to make
till They made
        you and me!

Clovers on hilltops,
a sparrow in flight,
a fox safe and snug
on a September night,

An indigo sapphire,
the storm winds that blow,
all life and creations
sprang from the same glow.

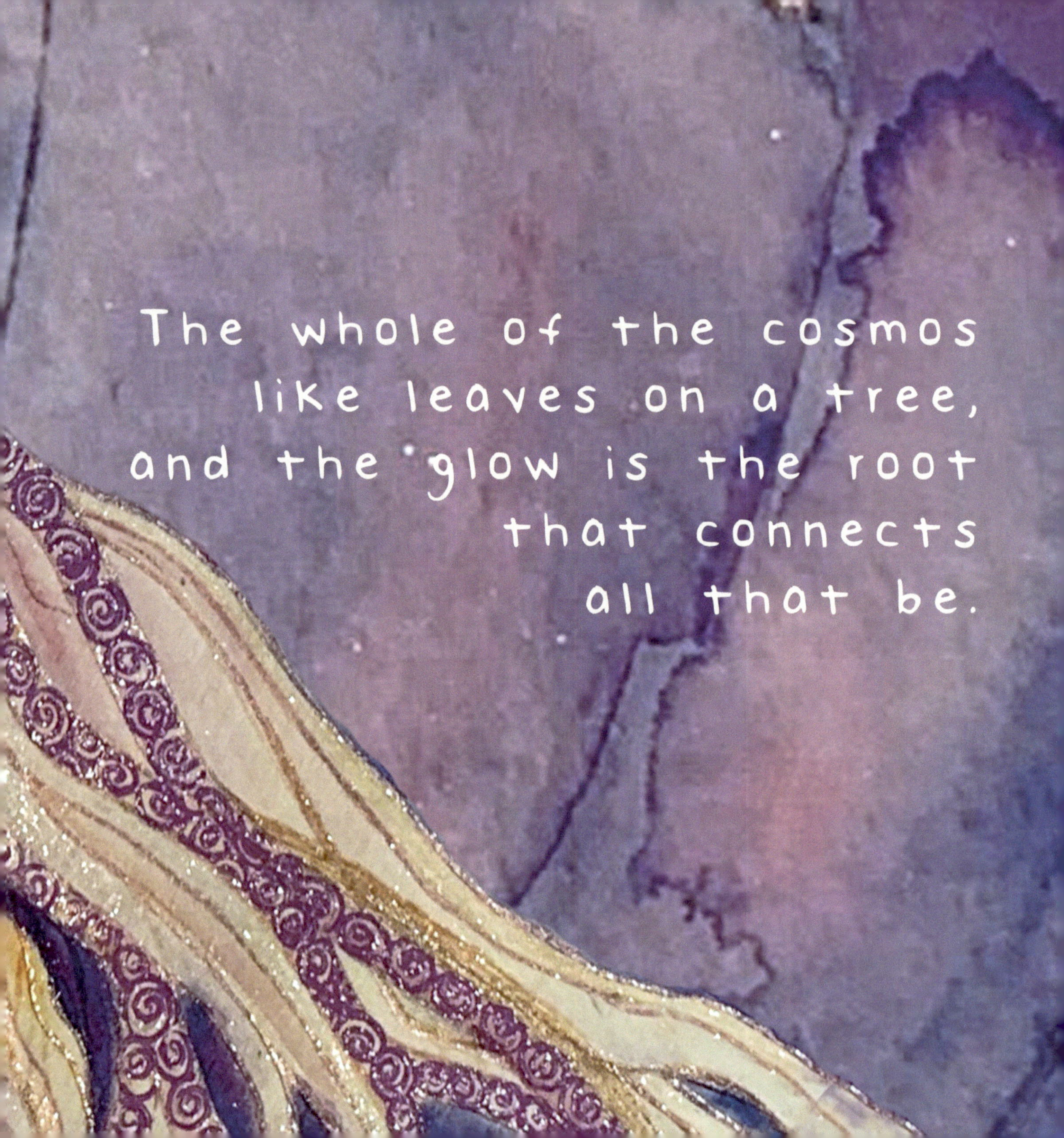

The whole of the cosmos
like leaves on a tree,
and the glow is the root
that connects
all that be.

So,
should you be outside
and meet someone new,
and you pause because
they look different
from you,

Lay down your fear,
trust what your
heart knows...

We all share
this gift of life
known as the

glw.

About the author

Shannon Cannon is a pediatric registered nurse who lives in Arizona with her husband, Cole, their six children (counting one in heaven), one dog and one tortoise.

Her hobbies include sewing, painting, practicing piano, aerial silks, writing poems, camping, and traveling the whole world to learn and see as much as she can.